Masterpiece

by Nathan Metcalf

Baker's Plays
7611 Sunset Blvd.
Los Angeles, CA 90042
bakersplays.com

MASTERPIECE was created for the Minnesota State High School League One-Act Play competition. It was first performed January 29, 2005 at St. Michael-Albertville High School, and subsequently performed at Dassel-Cokato High School, and the College of St. Catherine in St. Paul, MN. All three performances received the highest rankings possible.

The cast was as follows:

THE ARTIST . . . . Anna Posthumus
BLUE . . . . Jacob Bebeau
PINK . . . . Kate Bridal
PURPLE . . . . Ashley Budde
GOLD . . . . Shaylee Carlson
RED . . . . Derek Holm
YELLOW . . . . Liz McAllister
GREEN . . . . Steven Posthumus
ORANGE . . . . Robert Swansen
MOLLY . . . . Megan Selvig

Crew: Holly Conwell, Toni Berning, Bekki Jossart, Cory Kessler, Andrew Evans, Ben Glasser.

The show was directed by Jox Metcalf.

Costumes were created by Linda Metcalf. The set was designed by Nathan Metcalf and created by Roger Bovee.

The play is dedicated to Frances, who taught me to sing for the joy of it,
and to Jolene, who fell in love with a daydreamer.

(The set is designed to look like an artist's studio, with no relation to size. Stage Right we see three paint cans of varying heights with paint slopped around the rims, forming a step unit. Upstage Center is a tube of acrylic paint, high enough to sit or stand on. Upstage Right is a jar with 8-foot paint brushes sticking out of it. Next to it is a sittable pink eraser. Stage Right features a box of crayons. Littered about the floor are gigantic sheets of paper with a child's drawings on them.)

I. PROLOGUE: IMAGINE A CANVAS

(In the blackout, we hear the first strains of music. A scrim is lit in purple, showing the silhouette of the set. Lights down. Music plays on. Seconds later the scrim lights come up [red], revealing the cast in silhouette in an artistic design. This holds for two or three seconds, then lights down again.)

(Scrim lights up, [blue]. Two people are posed in silhouette as Grant Wood's American Gothic. *Lights down.)*

(Scrim lights up, [green] We see actors in silhouette as the evolutionary chart. Lights Down.)

(Scrim lights up, [gold]. Two actors in silhouette form Leonardo DaVinci's The Vitruvian Man. *Lights Down.)*

(Full stage lights up. The actors are stationed in various places around the stage. They are dressed in black, with each one wearing a brightly-colored artist's smock and beret. One by one they break out of tableau to speak their lines.)

BLUE. Imagine a canvas…

GOLD. A shape…

ORANGE. A few lines. A dab of color.

RED. Imagine a painting.

GREEN. With form.

PINK. Rhythm.

PURPLE. Harmony.

ORANGE. Motif.

PURPLE. With a purpose.

YELLOW. *(as actors pose as abstract versions of art from each painter)* Picture a Picasso.
A Rembrandt.
Renoir.
Van Gogh.
Cassat.
A Monet, a Reubens.
Chagall.

BLUE. *(giving* **YELLOW** *a kiss as in the painting,* The Kiss*)* A Klimt.

GOLD. *(as actors pose as each of the paintings)* Imagine a lady with a mysterious smile. The creation of Adam. The birth of a Venus, A night full of stars. A field of sunflowers. A man locked in an eternal scream.
Imagine Art.

PURPLE. Picture Art. Picture life, picture joy.

BLUE. Picture man's triumph over boredom and uncertainty.

RED. Picture man's quest for enlightenment. Picture…a good way to spend a Sunday afternoon. Picture Art.

ALL. Art. *(The word echoes throughout the cast.)*

GREEN. "Art is truth." – Vincent Van Gogh

BLUE. "Art is not the truth, but a lie that makes us see the truth." – Pablo Picasso

PINK. "I found I could say things with color and shapes that I couldn't say any other way…things I had no words for." – Georgia O'Keeffe

ORANGE. "Art is not what you see, but what you make others see." – Edgar Degas

RED. "Art is either plagiarism or revolution." – Paul Gaugin

PURPLE. "Every artist regardless of talent has one great masterpiece, one work which in his mind stands far beyond the rest. Whether or not the rest of the world agrees doesn't change a thing. To the artist, it remains a masterpiece." – Rene Magritte

YELLOW. This is the story of an Artist,

*(****THE ARTIST*** *enters dressed in white. She has a white bow in her hair and is full of energy.)*

and her struggle to find that masterpiece.

GOLD. Her journey to discover that for which we are all looking. Her –

ALL. Masterpiece.

II. THE ARTIST

*(Mood and music change. ****THE ARTIST*** *[at 6 years old] grabs an enormous crayon and begins drawing on one of the huge sheets of paper strewn about the floor.)*

BLUE. Imagine an Artist.

PURPLE. She could be your neighbor.

YELLOW. Your friend.

GOLD. The girl in line behind you in the grocery store.

GREEN. That girl who hit you with the volleyball in gym class.

BLUE. She's six years old here, so you may not recognize her.

RED. That's her, coloring a picture with her crayons. Crayola crayons. The big fat ones.

PINK. Purple.

BLUE. Red.

ORANGE. Blue.

RED. Yellow.

(These lines should NOT be spoken by their respectively colored characters.)

BLUE. That's her, drawing anemic cars and anorexic animals.

(The pictures are lifted off the floor to reveal **THE ARTIST***'s drawings.)*

PINK. Drawing Mommy and Daddy and the puppy too.

ORANGE. And always, her best friend Molly.

*(***MOLLY*** enters. She is a 2-dimensional little girl that has clearly been drawn by a 6-year old. Throughout the scene she stands alongside* **THE ARTIST** *and interacts silently.)*

PURPLE. *(lifting a picture)* "Molly and a Fire Engine."

GOLD. *(same)* "Molly and the Mailman."

YELLOW. "Molly and a Can of Peaches."

GREEN. Molly and a Monkey Wearing Roller Skates.

(Pause, they all look at **THE ARTIST.***)*

THE ARTIST. Because that way the bears can't catch him. Duh.

GREEN. *(deadpan, as if it's the title of the painting)* "Molly and a Monkey Wearing Roller Skates Because That Way the Bears Can't Catch Him…Duh."

LITTLE BOY (ORANGE). Teacher! Teacher! She's coloring outside the lines.

TEACHER (PINK). She always colors outside the lines.

THE ARTIST. Staying inside the lines is boring. Sometimes horses run outside their corrals. Sometimes cars drive on the grass. Sometimes my soup spills outside the bowl. So why do I have to stay in the lines?

TEACHER. Because staying in the lines gets you a gold star.

THE ARTIST. But going outside the lines gives you orange hair, or green skin, or purple puppies. And those are much more fun than a gold star.

YELLOW. And if she didn't like where the lines were, she drew new ones. She drew everything she saw. She drew ON everything she saw. When she ran out of paper, she switched to tables, walls, Daddy's briefcase…Daddy.

*(During this exchange, **THE ARTIST** grabs an enormous crayon and writes on the wall. As she draws, a ribbon pulls out of the crayon tip to leave its mark. Halfway across the wall, she switches to a dull crayon of another color, draws another line, stops, peels the paper off the crayon, and continues drawing.)*

PINK. Then one day, Mommy and Daddy caught her writing on the walls. The Artist was afraid of what Mommy and Daddy would say. For one thing the form was all wrong, and she didn't capture the highlights and the shadows quite right.

BLUE. But instead of scolding her, they framed her art and showed it to all of the neighbors.

ORANGE. And they promised to take her to the zoo.

ARTIST. Can I bring Molly?

RED. Of course she could.

GOLD. Molly was her best friend. A crayon-drawing that came to life one bored Tuesday morning.

PINK. Just because The Artist was the only one who could see Molly, it didn't make her any less real.

RED. Together, their favorite thing in the world was going to the zoo.

*(The actors create animals on stage, while **MOLLY** and **THE ARTIST** watch and giggle. **THE ARTIST** draws each of the animals on a sketch pad.)*

PINK. First she drew the tigers. *(Lights up on the tigers.)*

THE ARTIST. *(crossing to another part of the stage)* Ooh, Molly look – Flamingos! *(Lights up on the flamingos.)*

PINK. Then they saw the wolves! *(Lights up on an empty portion of the stage.)* Come to think of it, nobody ever really sees the wolves, do they? But The Artist drew them anyway.

THE ARTIST. *(Lights up on the giraffe.)* A giraffe!

*(**RED** takes a 2-dimensional cut-out of a zoo animal and places it on an empty easel Upstage Right. It remains in view throughout the rest of the show.)*

PINK. And when they got home, The Artist and Molly colored pictures of every animal they saw. Every fish, every bird, and every ant.

(**GREEN** *enters downstage with an easel [and canvas].*)

GREEN. Time passed, as it does. Molly said goodbye, The Artist grew up, and her crayons were traded in for pencils, paints, and colored chalks.

(**MOLLY** *exits.* **THE ARTIST** *removes the white bow from her hair and begins drawing on the canvas. From this point onward, whenever* **THE ARTIST** *finishes a piece of art, she "signs" it with a flourish and two dots.*)

RED. She experimented with clay.

(**RED** *sits on all fours.* **THE ARTIST** *sits on him like a work bench and works an imaginary potter's wheel.*)

GOLD. She experimented with sculpture.

(**THE ARTIST** *poses* **GOLD** *like a mannequin.*)

YELLOW. She tried her hand at things more avant-garde and surreal.

(*Pause as they try to figure out what that is. Then some strike odd poses; two throw giant fruit to one another; another waltzes with an inflatable Godzilla; someone walks across the stage playing the tuba, weird noises are made, Someone says "There's a penguin in my eye!" or something equally bizarre. Then it all stops abruptly.*)

THE ARTIST. Some ideas worked better than others.

(*Dejected, all but* **THE ARTIST** *pout their way offstage.*)

GREEN. But it was in painting that The Artist truly found her calling.

PINK. She loved the intensity of the colors.

BLUE. The ease of the brushstroke.

ORANGE. The smell of a wet canvas.

YELLOW. The ability to capture her thoughts like no other medium could.

RED. She wanted to spend the rest of her life painting.

PINK. Time passed, as it does, and The Artist painted all through high school and all through college, when finally the day came. The Big Day. Graduation Day.

(The actors line up like expectant graduates. The Headmaster places a long, white scarf on **THE ARTIST***, and gives her a sketch pad and a paintbrush.* **THE ARTIST** *wears this scarf for the remainder of the play.)*

PURPLE. The headmaster clapped her on the shoulder, gave her a paint brush and a blank white canvas, saying,

HEADMASTER (BLUE). It's time. Go out and paint. The world is waiting for your Masterpiece!

THE ARTIST. My Masterpiece. I like the sound of that.

HEADMASTER. So what are you waiting for? Get to it!

ALL. *(ad lib)* Yeah! Get to it! *(etc.)* *(They exit, noisily cheering her on.)*

THE ARTIST. Yeah! I'll get to it! I'll paint…*(pause)*…What if I…*(pause)*…*(long pause)* But what do I paint? *(looks around the stage, now devoid of actors)* Oh sure, NOW they shut up.

III. BUSINESS

(Music and mood change. A woman strolls by walking her dog. **THE ARTIST** *watches, giggles, and sketches what she sees. Montage of people passing by doing various everyday things,* **THE ARTIST** *sketches each one and throws the paper aside. Eventually someone stops to watch over her shoulder.)*

PASSERBY (RED). Say, that's pretty good. How much you want for it?

THE ARTIST. How much? Oh, no, it's not for sale. It's just a rough draft. I thought maybe it could be my Masterpiece, but…that one wasn't it.

PASSERBY. But it's still pretty good. You should go into business.

THE ARTIST. Business?

PASSERBY. Yes, business! My cousin runs a business two

towns over. She's looking for painters like yerself. With talent like yours, you could go straight to the top.

YELLOW. The top! Not a bad place to go. Perhaps she could create her Masterpiece in the business world. So she collected her things and went to see The Boss.

(The **BOSS** *enters with a large dollar bill tucked under her arm. She's all business, barely pausing to even acknowledge* **THE ARTIST***. She fiddles with imaginary knobs and adjusts imaginary equipment.)*

BOSS (PINK). Welcome! Welcome! I was told you'd be coming. I've heard great things about you, so don't let me down, kid, don't let me down. We run a straight 4-40 shift here with a 15 every 3 hours. You'll be in Sector 14d, and your locker is on the Green concourse. My office is Sector W 17, but if you get lost, go see Margie in 56D, who will give you the proper forms to fill out. Plant runs until the whistle blows. No painting outside the lines. Here are some forms to fill out in triplicate and deliver to Frank in 46L before your shift starts – *(looks at watch)* oh, about now-ish. Good luck.

(Dance Sequence – The workers come in with gigantic paint brushes [two workers to each brush] and perform a very precise, synchronized sequence of movements to the music, their actions akin to painting something on a large scale. **THE ARTIST** *fumbles with holding a large brush by herself and tries to mimic their movements, without much success. Over the movements, the* **WORKERS** *throw out the following lines with overly chipper enthusiasm, while* **THE ARTIST** *tries [unsuccessfully] to get their attention.)*

WORKER 1 (ORANGE). How was your weekend, Shirley?

WORKER 2 (PURPLE). Just great. We took the kids to the lake.

ARTIST. Excuse me, but –

WORKER 3 (GREEN). So, Phyllis, did you catch the game yesterday?

WORKER 4 (GOLD). Sure did! That Hoineroinken is awesome!

THE ARTIST. Pardon me – Am I doing this right?

WORKER 5 (BLUE). Hey Scooter, were your hours off last week?

WORKER 6 (RED). I dunno, Skip. Better ask Margie.

THE ARTIST. *(to herself, trying to get the movement right)* So it's jump, then move …

WORKER 3. Look out, New Kid!

(**THE ARTIST** *is nearly run over by one of the brushes.*)

WORKER 4. So the doctor said I need to have to have surgery on my knee.

WORKER 2. My sister had that done. I tell you, I've never seen such a gangrenous patella.

THE ARTIST. But what are we –

WORKER 1. The Boss has been riding me to get my fourth quarter numbers up.

WORKER 6. Oh, man, that's tough.

WORKER 3. So then someone took my donut from the break room.

(*They all stop at once and look at their watches.*)

ALL. Break Time!

(*The* **WORKERS** *move upstage center and take a rest. Even on break, they are still creepily chipper.*)

THE ARTIST. So what are we painting?

WORKER 5. Dollar Bills!

THE ARTIST. Do we get to paint anything else?

WORKER 1. No ma'am, just dollar bills.

THE ARTIST. What? All day?

WORKER 2. Of course! Why would you want to paint anything else? Money is the only thing that matters around here.

ALL WORKERS. Ain't it great??!

BOSS. Back to work!

(*Dance sequence resumes with* **THE ARTIST** *becoming increasingly bored and disillusioned. She has the movements down now and performs them in time, but with apathy. The* **WORKERS** *remain chipper as ever. The following lines are spoken with the exact same inflection as before.*)

WORKER 1. How was your weekend, Shirley?

WORKER 2. Just great. We took the kids to the lake.

WORKER 3. So, Phyllis, did you catch the game yesterday?

WORKER 4. Sure did! That Hoineroinken is awesome!

WORKER 5. Hey Scooter, were your hours off last week?

WORKER 6. I dunno, Skip. Better ask Margie.

> *(In frustration,* **THE ARTIST** *screams and runs out.)*

> *(The* **WORKERS** *file out. Light and mood change. The* **BOSS** *takes the giant dollar bill from under her arm and places it on an empty easel next to the zoo icon Upstage Right.)*

YELLOW. Dejected, The Artist wandered the streets. Clearly she would not be able to paint a masterpiece under those conditions.

ORANGE. There was no variety. No meaning. No…art. This simply would not do. Was she not, after all, an artist? She walked for days searching for anything that could be the subject of her masterpiece. As she walked, she came across an old woman praying.

IV. CHURCH

THE ARTIST. May I join you?

> *(The* **OLD WOMAN** *nods and pats the ground next to her. They pray in silence. The* **OLD WOMAN** *looks at* **THE ARTIST,** *concerned.)*

OLD WOMAN (YELLOW). You look troubled.

THE ARTIST. I am. I'm afraid I won't be able to find my masterpiece.

OLD WOMAN. You're young. *(gives her a comforting pat on the knee)* Give it time. It will come. *(a beat)* But if you're looking for inspiration, there's always…*(points)*

> *(An enormous stained glass window appears on the scrim. A church bell is heard, tolling once.)*

PURPLE. She pointed to the old grey church in the town square.

GOLD. The old woman was right. Perhaps her inspiration just needed to be a bit more…divine. She thanked her fellow pilgrim and headed toward the church. At the door, she was met by two men dressed in black. Their calm and welcoming demeanor put her instantly at ease.

(Two **PRIESTS** *enter in black cassocks. Their voices are tranquil, but firm. They aren't cartoony, but are genuinely concerned, and genuinely trying to help. One carries a thick tome.)*

PRIEST 1 (BLUE). Come in.

PRIEST 2 (GREEN). Please.

PRIEST 1. Sit where you like.

GOLD. They left The Artist alone with her thoughts. Religious icons filled the cathedral, filling her senses and instilling a peace inside her.

THE ARTIST. This could give me the tranquility I need to find my Masterpiece.

PURPLE. She thought of Michelangelo and Bernini and all of the work they did for the church. She could do the same. Immediately, she grabbed a brush and started painting.

(The **PRIESTS** *approach.)*

PRIEST 2. Pardon me, miss, but what are you doing?

THE ARTIST. Oh, sorry, I was just capturing my thoughts.

PRIEST 1. Ah, I see. I'm terribly sorry, but we can't allow you to do that here. *(very calmly takes* **THE ARTIST***'s sketch pad away)*

THE ARTIST. I'm sorry?

PRIEST 2. Yes, painting is not allowed here. It's forbidden by the Book of Rules

THE ARTIST. The Book of Rules?

PRIEST 1. Yes.

PRIEST 2. That kind of artistic endeavor detracts from our true purpose here.

THE ARTIST. Which is?

PRIEST 1. To study the Book of Rules.

PRIEST 2. Among other things.

PRIEST 1. Yes. Among other things.

PRIEST 2. *(trying to help)* But if you like, you can stay here and make stained glass windows.

PRIEST 1. You see, they're functional. They serve a purpose.

PURPLE. The Artist thought about this for a minute. While not what she had in mind, she could still create a masterpiece with colored glass. Her mind raced with different color combinations she could try. Shapes flooded her imagination. She could do this. She could do this well. It wasn't perfect, but it was good enough. And sometimes "good enough" is good enough.

THE ARTIST. Gentlemen,

PURPLE. She responded.

THE ARTIST. Show me the way.

(They cross to where 3 actors use stylized movement to replicate making windows.)

GOLD. They led her to a workshop where other workers were cutting the glass. Heat from the ovens was intense, but her newly found sense of purpose excited her, and kept her from noticing anything else.

PRIEST 1. Now before you begin, remember, what you are doing, you are not doing for your personal glory.

PRIEST 2. You are doing it for the Church.

THE ARTIST. I can agree to that.

PRIEST 1. And you may not work on Sundays.

PRIEST 2. Or after Sundown.

THE ARTIST. Okay.

PRIEST 1. Only use the colors which we provide for you.

PRIEST 2. Your first window must be completed within 40 days.

PRIEST 1 Only use the shapes which we provide for you.

PRIEST 2. When on a break, you may only read the Book of Rules.

PRIEST 1. Only use the patterns which we provide for you.

PRIEST 2. And no fraternizing with the other workers.

PRIEST 1. Only use the tools which we provide for you.

(Uneasy, **THE ARTIST** *gets up and leaves the priests babbling. They don't notice her leave.)*

PRIEST 2. You may not eat or drink in the workshop.

PRIEST 1. Above all else, the Book of Rules is always correct.

(They trail offstage, still talking. **PURPLE** *takes a stained glass window and places it on an empty easel Upstage Center.)*

PINK. The Artist slipped out of the church unnoticed and kept walking until she was out of town. This couldn't be it, she thought. A masterpiece can't be that structured, that laid out. Or that prone to compromise.

GOLD. Religion is faith. And faith lives in *people*, not buildings or rules. Good art doesn't follow the rules. Great artists become great by NOT following the rules. She couldn't settle. Suddenly her "good enough" wasn't so good anymore. But was she good enough to create a masterpiece? She had already tried twice.

PINK. And failed twice. And was now facing a long dark road ahead of her. Taking a deep breath, and sighing a deep sigh, she trudged on.

V. THE DAYDREAMER

(Music and mood change. Actors simulate a park. Girls playing jump rope, an old woman knitting, feeding pigeons, etc. **THE ARTIST** *hunches over to feed some ducks. The* **DAYDREAMER** *enters running, zipping right in front of her.)*

PINK. Three towns over, she stopped to feed some ducks, when she was nearly run over by a young man.

THE ARTIST. *(brushing herself off)* You really should watch where you're going.

DAYDREAMER (ORANGE). Why? It's more fun to watch everything else along the way. Take those ducks, for instance. If I was watching where I was going, I'd never notice *that* one is three times fatter than the others. Or that that guy duck right there has it real bad for the female over there.

YELLOW. He gave a deep, overly important bow, and introduced himself as a daydreamer.

DAYDREAMER. Are you a daydreamer too?

THE ARTIST. I'm an artist.

DAYDREAMER. Same thing.

PURPLE. The Artist couldn't help but like him. She came back to the park the next day and watched him playing jump rope with some kids on the playground. The next day, she watched as he did nothing but look at clouds all afternoon.

PINK. It was after the third day that he asked to walk her home.

GREEN. Time passed, as it does. Autumn came and went, and she saw a lot more of the Daydreamer. When he wasn't looking, she painted pictures of him.

RED. Playing with a stray dog.

GOLD. Swimming in the fountain.

PURPLE. Reading the newspaper on a park bench.

BLUE. Falling asleep in her lap on the picnic blanket.

GOLD. There was something childlike about his curiosity about everyone and everything that passed his eye. His energy was endless. And infectious.

YELLOW. It didn't take long for her to fall in love with him. Real love. Not the mad, infatuous crush of a schoolgirl, but honest love.

> (*The* **DAYDREAMER** *gives* **THE ARTIST** *a white beret, which she wears for the remainder of the play.*)

PURPLE. The kind of love that inspired artists like Renoir and Cassat.

PINK. The kind that inspired Reubens to paint his angels.

GREEN. The kind of love to drive Van Gough mad enough to cut off his own ear.

PINK. And he returned her love every chance he got. He brought dandelions to place in her hair.

BLUE. He read her plays, using different voices for each of the characters.

GREEN. He cooked soup for her when the days got colder.

PINK. She loved him so, and filled canvas upon canvas with pictures of him. Colors swirled through her brush. Images, Shapes, Lines. She felt free, uninhibited. ALIVE!

PURPLE. Love felt divine. It provided her with the inspiration she needed. Could this be it? The greatest cliché in the history of the world? Who would have thought?

PINK. After a year of this romantic bliss, it hit her. This was it. This was the time. Time to start the Masterpiece.

*(***RED*** and ***GOLD*** enter with a series of paintings of The Daydreamer in various surroundings)*

GOLD. The Artist went into the room that had now become her studio. There she found all the paintings she had made of the Daydreamer.

RED. Here was the one of him rowing the boat and singing off-key.

GOLD. Here was the one of him dancing in the snow.

RED. The one of him pretending to be a penguin.

PURPLE. She giggled to herself, then looked at the pictures again. Something was wrong. Something was missing from this picture.

RED. And this one.

GOLD. And the next and the next.

PURPLE. And all of them. Something was missing.

THE ARTIST. *(long pause)* Me.

BLUE. Hundreds of pictures of the Daydreamer, but she hadn't painted herself into a single one.

*(***THE ARTIST*** crosses to where the ***DAYDREAMER*** has fallen asleep. She sits beside him, stroking his hair.)*

PURPLE. Was this how she saw herself? Unimportant?

BLUE. She thought back over the past year. Everything she had done was for him, not for *THEM*.

PINK. But she loved him, didn't she? And he loved her back.

YELLOW. But something wasn't right. She didn't know what was supposed to happen, but she knew this wasn't it.

(*THE ARTIST stands, keeping her eyes on the sleeping* **DAYDREAMER**. *Her gaze shifts to her sketchpad. She drops it like it's hot, and runs to the other side of the stage. Through this next segment,* **ORANGE** *takes a painting of The Daydreamer and places it on an easel Upstage Left beside the other icons.*)

PURPLE. In a panic, she ran. The Artist ran and ran.

BLUE. And ran and ran and ran.

GOLD. She didn't know what she was running from.

GREEN. Perhaps she was running from the Daydreamer.

RED. From her life.

BLUE. From herself.

YELLOW. Perhaps she was just running because it was the only thing that made sense.

PURPLE. She ran and ran.

ALL. And ran and ran and ran.

ORANGE. After days of running, she collapsed against a tree, exhausted. And it was there she fell asleep.

VI. DREAM SEQUENCE

(*THE ARTIST sits against the box of crayons and falls asleep. Light and mood change. Stage goes into black-light. Only* **THE ARTIST** *is visible, due to her white clothing. It is important that she is still wearing her beret and scarf.*)

GOLD. She dreamt of nothing. Of nothingness. Shapes whirled past her head. Colors. Lines

(*Two or three giant tangram shapes fly-by. As do yellow and orange ribbons.* **THE ARTIST** *stands and watches the traffic. We see three glowing balls juggle themselves past. The last shape, a small triangle, stops in front of* **THE ARTIST**, *and looks at her curiously before flying on its way.*)

ORANGE. The Artist saw a spot on the horizon. It grew in size until she could make out the shape of a boat on the water.

(The seven tangram pieces form the shape of a clipper ship then move in harmony across the stage.)

BLUE. The boat sailed past, as though The Artist herself was nothing more than a lighthouse keeping watch over the shore.

PURPLE. Trying to get a bearing on her surroundings, The Artist explored further.

(The boat silently shifts to a puppy who nips at **THE ARTIST**'s *heels.)*

RED. Let's play, said the puppy.

THE ARTIST. I don't have time to play.

RED. Please! It'll be so much fun.

THE ARTIST. I'm sure it would, but I really don't have time to play.

RED. Are you busy?

THE ARTIST. I'm busy.

RED. Are you too busy?

THE ARTIST. I'm too busy.

RED. Are you too busy wasting your life trying to look for your masterpiece?

THE ARTIST. I'm too busy wasting – What?? How do you know about me?

PINK. I know more than you think. Does this look familiar?

(The puppy shifts to the image of a painter, whose brush moves up and down in slow rhythm.)

THE ARTIST. A painter. So if you know so much about me, what am I going to do next?

PINK. That is up to you.

(The painter shifts to the image of a man's head. The jaw moves when he speaks.)

THE ARTIST. But if I'm wasting my life looking for my Masterpiece, what should I do?

GREEN. Stop looking.

THE ARTIST. Stop looking? That's it? That's the answer to the riddle of the ancients? Just give up because it's all hopeless?

GREEN. You're not listening. I didn't say give up. I said stop *looking.* You won't find it. Just let it happen. It will find you.

THE ARTIST. What's that supposed to mean?

GREEN. You're looking too hard. And you're painting for all the wrong reasons. Painting to make money. Painting to serve the church. Painting to immortalize someone. *(a beat)* When you were six, what was your favorite thing in the world?

THE ARTIST. *(fondly)* That's easy. Coloring.

GREEN. Ah! Now *why* did you color?

THE ARTIST. Because it – *(realizing)* Because it was fun.

GREEN. Because it was fun!

(The face changes to the shape of a juggler.)

BLUE. Exactly. What happened to the fun? Art doesn't need a purpose. It's at its best when it's created out of sheer bliss. Sheer joy.

THE ARTIST. *(nodding)* I get it. "Sing for the joy of it. Your supper is free."

BLUE. Even when you're at your darkest and most depressed. Paint then, too. Paint what you feel. Paint *because* you feel. It will still be fun.

GOLD. Suddenly everything made sense. A great weight had been lifted off her shoulders. She was six again.

(The pieces scatter, twisting and swirling slowly.)

YELLOW. Images flooded her mind of new things to paint. Colors intermingled with lines, shapes. New harmonies floated around her head. *(She takes off her scarf and twirls it in the blacklight, painting across the sky.)*

RED. Perspectives and angles.

PURPLE. Rhymes and textures.

GREEN. Art. The art came back.

THE ARTIST. *(fascinated)* Who ARE you? WHAT are you?

PURPLE. A Friend.

*(The pieces separate to reveal **MOLLY**.)*

THE ARTIST. Molly! You did …all this?

MOLLY (VOICED BY PURPLE). Uh-huh. I've always been with you, watching you. You had me worried there for a second. But you seem to have found your way.

THE ARTIST. I just needed a good guide.

(a beat)

MOLLY. So…I suppose you'll be waking up soon, then, huh?

THE ARTIST. I'm in no hurry. What do you say we go to the zoo one more time?

(The shapes form a wolf in the spot where they should have been at the zoo.)

THE ARTIST. Look, Molly, the wolves!

(One by one, the pieces fly off of the wolf and off stage. The two smallest triangles stay onstage and settle near the Upstage Left icons.)

THE ARTIST. Goodbye Molly. I'll see you when I wake up.

*(They wave goodbye, and **THE ARTIST** returns to the spot where she fell asleep.)*

VII. MASTERPIECE

PINK. The Artist awoke relaxed, refreshed, and renewed.

RED. She also realized she was a long, long way from home.

THE ARTIST. Oh well,

RED. She said.

THE ARTIST. I'll just have to take the scenic route home.

RED. Which she did.

PURPLE. On the way, she picked flowers, painted pictures for total strangers, and realized she missed the Day-dreamer.

YELLOW. She did indeed love him. And while she did paint hundreds of pictures of him, none of them was a masterpiece. But they were still pretty good.

GOLD. And they were painted out of love, joy and bliss.

GREEN. About half way home, she passed a sail maker, who had just discarded a large scrap of canvas. Feeling inspired by the night air she took out a brush and painted a sky on the canvas.

(*Music swells.* **THE ARTIST** *sees it all come together. An enormous artist's palette flies in and settles Stage Right.*)

THE ARTIST. (*pointing to the icon on the easel Upstage Right.*) The Zoo!

(**RED** *takes the zoo icon off the easel and holds it beside the palette.*)

RED. Then, splashes of color. A sprinkle of light.

THE ARTIST. The Factory!

(**PINK** *takes the dollar bill icon and holds it beside the others. This continues with all of the other icons, forming the Masterpice Downstage Right.* **THE ARTIST** *"air paints" the Masterpiece while the pieces fly into place like a mosaic, or jigsaw puzzle.*)

PURPLE. Images flowed out of her – the factory, the church, Molly, the Daydreamer, The Zoo, the Dream – All of it flew onto the canvas along with her sweat.

PINK. Her frustrations.

BLUE. And her ambitions.

GOLD. Finally, she had found her Masterpiece!

(*Music reaches a triumphant finish. Then a mood change. Music fades out completely. The following takes place with minimal movement.*)

YELLOW. She painted for three days straight. On the fourth day, she stepped back to get one final look at her work.

(**THE ARTIST** *backs away and drops to the floor, staring at the Masterpiece. Long beat before the* **DAYDREAMER** *enters. He stands looking at the Masterpiece.* **THE ARTIST** *doesn't see him.*)

DAYDREAMER. Looks good.

THE ARTIST. (*not taking her eyes off the painting*) Thanks.

DAYDREAMER. Really good.

THE ARTIST. *(finally looking at him)* Thanks.

(a beat)

DAYDREAMER. I missed you.

THE ARTIST. I'm sorry. I had to go.

DAYDREAMER. I know.

THE ARTIST. *(Stands. Goes to him.)* I was on my way back –

(soft music underscores)

DAYDREAMER. I know. *(pause)* I followed you. You're worth chasing after.

(**THE ARTIST** *smiles. The* **DAYDREAMER** *hands her the sketchpad.)*

Here. You dropped this.

THE ARTIST. *(gesturing to the Masterpiece)* I kind of got side-tracked.

DAYDREAMER. I see that.

(They stand silently for a beat, looking at the Master-piece, holding hands.)

It's missing something.

THE ARTIST. What?

DAYDREAMER. Here.

(He pulls her over to stand in front of the Masterpiece, posing her like a mannequin, then gives her one of the oversized brushes.)

It's missing the most important part. *(stepping back)* There. *Now* it's a masterpiece.

(a beat)

GOLD. "Every artist regardless of talent has one great mas-terpiece."

PINK. "One work which in her mind stands far beyond the rest."

GREEN. "Whether or not the rest of the world agrees doesn't change a thing."

THE ARTIST. "To The Artist, it remains a masterpiece."

(Slow fade. On the scrim, images appear one by one. The Mona Lisa, American Gothic, The Creation of Man, The Birth of Venus, The Vitruvian Man, then after a pause, a painted version of the Downstage Right tableau with **THE ARTIST** *at the center.)*

(fade to black)

(curtain)

PRODUCTION NOTES:

Masterpiece contains abstract visual elements that require additional explanation. What follows are notes on how these visual elements were tackled in the original production. These are merely suggestions, as directors are free to explore other possible solutions.

SCRIM

Masterpiece works best with a full cyclorama or flat scrim. If necessary, a portable scrim can be set up in the back, but this is discouraged, as it cuts off playing space. It is also most advisable to close black curtains in front of the scrim, as an exposed scrim creates problems during the blacklight sequence.

MOLLY

Molly is played by a live actor, wearing a two-dimensional costume, constructed of thin plywood attached to a harness. Molly's head, similarly, attaches to a helmet. Her arms are jointed at the shoulders, elbows, and wrists, to allow for maximum mobility. Her legs are likewise jointed. Both body and head are painted to look like a child's drawing of a little girl. The actor playing Molly doesn't speak, but accompanies The Artist where necessary.

DRAWINGS ON OVERSIZED PAPER

At the top of the show, the giant pieces of paper cover the stage. They already have the drawings on them ("Molly and a Can of Peaches", etc), thus avoiding the need for The Artist to draw them live each performance.

TANGRAM PIECES / DREAM SEQUENCE

A Tangram is a puzzle consisting of seven pieces (tans): two large triangles, one medium triangle, two small triangles, one square, and one parallelogram. These can be arranged to form thousands of two-dimensional images. There are many resources, both in print and online, for finding patterns and designs that can be created with these seven pieces. In the dream sequence, seven oversized pieces are fitted to broom handles, one actor to each piece. The pieces are spun, twirled, and moved laterally to make the images that The Artist sees and interacts with. The pieces are painted with fluorescent paint so they can be seen under the blacklight. The actors wear black, so they cannot.

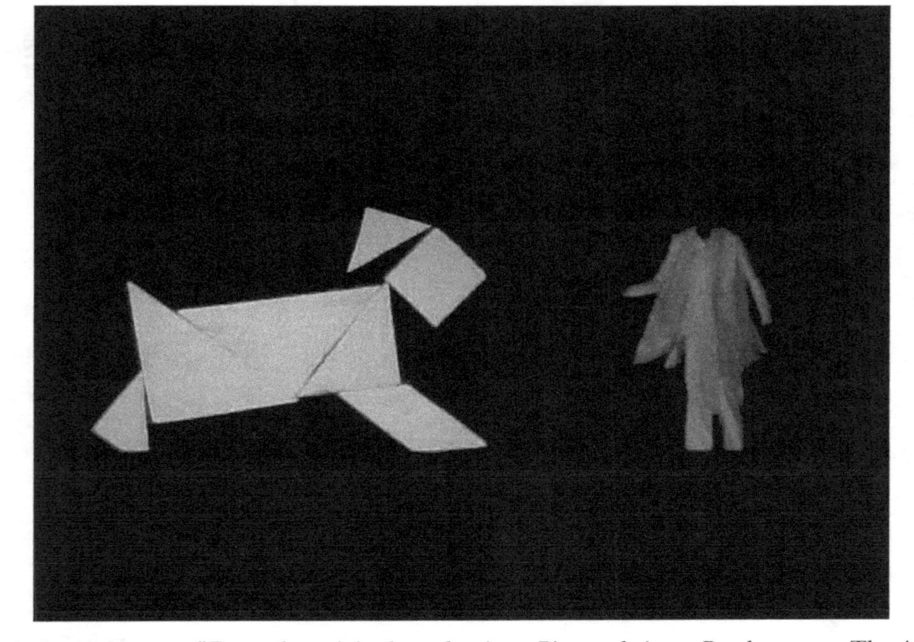

"Let's play! said the puppy." From the original production. Pictured: Anna Posthumus as The Artist
Photo used by permission of the author

www.ingramcontent.com/pod-product-compliance
Lightning Source LLC
Chambersburg PA
CBHW061107050726
47592CB00004B/1859